THE JUNGLE BOOK

Story written by Neil Morris

**Based upon The Walt Disney Company's
film of the same name**

**Hippo Books
Scholastic Publications Limited
London**

Scholastic Publications Ltd.,
10 Earlham Street, London WC2H 9RX, UK

Scholastic Inc.,
730 Broadway, New York, NY 10003, USA

Scholastic Canada Ltd.
123 Newkirk Road, Richmond Hill,
Ontario L4C 3G5, Canada

Ashton Scholastic Pty. Ltd.,
PO Box 579, Gosford, New South Wales,
Australia

Ashton Scholastic Ltd.,
165 Marua Road, Panmure, Auckland 6,
New Zealand

This edition first published by Scholastic Publications Limited, 1988 by
arrangement with The Walt Disney Company
© The Walt Disney Company 1988

ISBN 0 590 70992 5

Many strange legends are told about the jungles of India. But none is as strange as the story of a small boy named Mowgli.

It all began when the silence of the jungle was broken by an unfamiliar noise. Bagheera, a black panther, was walking beside the river when he heard the sound. He stopped, looked round, and saw that it was coming from a basket in a broken boat on the river bank. Bagheera went over and looked into the basket.

1

There, gurgling and kicking his legs, was a tiny baby. "This Man-cub must have nourishment, and soon," thought the panther. "Without a mother's care, he will not survive long in the jungle." Then an idea occurred to him. A family of wolves he knew had recently had a litter of cubs. Surely the mother wolf would look after the Man-cub?

Bagheera carried the basket to the wolves' cave. Putting it down near the entrance, he waited in the bushes. It was not long before mother wolf and her cubs came out to see what the strange noise was, for the baby was now crying at the top of his voice. As they peered into the basket in astonishment, Rama, the father of the wolfcubs, came over to see what it could be. He sniffed at the basket, looked in – and smiled. And mother wolf carefully carried the basket into the cave.

This was how Mowgli, the Man-cub, came to be brought up by wolves. As the years passed, Bagheera often came to see how Mowgli was getting on. He saw that the Man-cub was a favourite with all the wolfcubs, and that he was happy. But Bagheera knew that one day Mowgli would have to go back to his own people.

When Mowgli was ten years old, the wolf elders had a special meeting. Shere Khan, the tiger, had come back to their part of the jungle, and the wolves feared for the Man-cub's safety. "Shere Khan will surely kill the boy, and all who try to protect him," said Akela, the pack leader. "Rama, it is my unpleasant duty to tell you that the Man-cub can no longer stay with the pack. He must leave at once."

Rama was horrified. "But he's like my own son," he cried. "And he surely could not live alone in the jungle."

Bagheera was listening in a nearby tree. "Perhaps I can be of help," he told Akela. "I know a Man-village where Mowgli will be safe. We have taken many walks together in the jungle, and I'm sure he'll go with me."

The wolf elders agreed, and Bagheera set out with Mowgli that very night. But the boy was soon tired. "Shouldn't we go home now?" he asked Bagheera. "This time we're not going back," Bagheera replied gently. "I'm taking you to a Man-village."

"But why?" cried the boy.

"Because Shere Khan has sworn to kill you," said Bagheera.

Mowgli could not understand this. "Kill me? Why?" he asked.

"Shere Khan hates Man," Bagheera replied, "and he will never allow you to grow into one!"

"But I don't want to go to the Man-village," Mowgli wailed. "I want to stay in the jungle. I'm not afraid of a tiger." Bagheera felt sorry for the boy, but he knew that he must do as agreed.

"We'll spend the night here," he said. "Things will look better in the morning." And with that he pushed Mowgli up a tall tree. Bagheera was tired himself, and lay down at once to sleep.

As Mowgli was sitting sulking, along slithered Kaa, a very
sneaky snake. "I sssay, what have we here? It'sss a Man-cub,"
the snake hissed. "Now go to sssleep – yesss, to *sssleep*!" As
Mowgli looked at the snake, his eyes began to be hypnotized.
"Sssleep, sssleep," hissed Kaa, wrapping his coils round
Mowgli.

The boy struggled to stay awake. "Bag. . .Bagheera!" he
called. The panther opened one sleepy eye and was horrified to
see Kaa. He quickly hit the snake's head with his paw; Mowgli
pushed his coils off the branch, and the snake fell to the
ground with a thud.

Next morning, Mowgli was awakened by a thunderous
noise. A booming voice shouted, "Up-two-three-four, up-
two-three-four . . ."

"A parade!" cried Mowgli, swinging down to the ground.

"Oh, no," moaned Bagheera sleepily. "The elephant
patrol!"

Bagheera was right. A herd of elephants was marching
through the jungle, their leader at the head and a baby
elephant at the rear. Mowgli was fascinated. Joining in at the
end, he asked the little one what they were doing.

"We're on dawn patrol!" came the proud reply. "You can
join in if you like. Just do as I do." So Mowgli got down on all
fours and marched behind the baby elephant. But when the
order came to turn, Mowgli was too slow and banged straight
into him.

"Company, halt!" bawled the leader, Colonel Hathi.

"Time for inspection," whispered the little one. Colonel Hathi came down the line, and at last reached Mowgli. The colonel was pleased to see a new recruit, but then he looked closer. "A Man-cub!" he bellowed. "This is treason! I'll have no Man-cub in my jungle!"

"It's not your jungle," Mowgli objected. Bagheera could see that there was trouble ahead. He quickly explained that he was taking Mowgli to the Man-village, and hurried him away.

"I'm not going to the Man-village!" Mowgli said stubbornly.

"You're going if I have to drag you every step of the way," said Bagheera. They argued on and on, until at last Bagheera's patience was exhausted.

"That's it," he said. "I've had enough. From now on you're on your own!" And with that Bagheera walked off.

Mowgli sat down and sulked. But he was not alone for long. A big brown bear came by, singing to himself. "Now, what have we here?" the bear laughed. "It looks like you need help, little fella, and old Baloo is here to look after you."

"Leave me alone," snapped Mowgli. But Baloo just laughed, and danced around the boy with his fists up. At last Mowgli could no longer resist a fight. As they circled round each other, Mowgli couldn't help smiling and Baloo taught him how to growl like a bear.

Bagheera was not far off, worrying about Mowgli. When he heard the growls, he bounded through the jungle towards them. He was relieved to see Baloo, and by this time Mowgli was sitting on the bear, tickling him.

"That's enough, Baloo," said Bagheera. "Mowgli's going back to the Man-village, right now." Baloo was shocked, and so too, of course, was the boy.

"I want to stay here with Baloo," cried Mowgli.

"Certainly you do," laughed Baloo. Bagheera could only watch and shake his head as Baloo went on teaching Mowgli to box, and then to sing and dance. At last they flopped into the river together and floated downstream, with Mowgli on Baloo's stomach.

Baloo was so happy, floating with his eyes closed, that he didn't even notice when a monkey hung down from a tree and snatched Mowgli. It was some time before the bear realized that the monkeys were throwing the boy from tree to tree. He got out of the river and chased after them, but it was no good. There was only one thing for it. "Bagheera!" Baloo yelled at the top of his booming voice.

The panther was there at once, regretting that he had ever let the Man-cub out of his sight. "Those mangy monkeys carried Mowgli off," Baloo explained.

Bagheera thought quickly. "The ancient ruins!" he said suddenly. "That's where they'll take him, to meet their leader, King Louie. We've no time to lose!"

   As usual, Bagheera was right. When they reached the
ancient ruins, they saw that Mowgli had been brought before
the ape king. Bagheera and Baloo hid and listened.
   "Word has reached my royal ear that you want to stay in the
jungle," said Louie. "Well, I'll help you if you'll help me."
   "I'll do anything to stay in the jungle," replied Mowgli.
"What do you want me to do?"
   "Just tell me the secret of Man's red fire," said Louie.
   "So that's what the scoundrel's after," Bagheera whispered.
   "But I don't know how to make fire," Mowgli told King
Louie.

Meanwhile, Baloo slipped away and made himself up to look like a giant ape. Bagheera had told him to create a disturbance so that he could snatch Mowgli, but this was ridiculous! At first the disguise worked, and King Louie and the other monkeys danced round the newcomer. But before Bagheera could grab Mowgli, Baloo's disguise fell off and there was suddenly a terrible silence.

Then pandemonium broke out. Louie grabbed Mowgli, Baloo grabbed him from Louie, a monkey grabbed him from Baloo, and so it went on till the ruins started to crumble and fall. Bagheera took the opportunity to run off with the Man-cub on his back, and Baloo followed him at top speed.

When they were safe, Bagheera put Mowgli down to rest and he was soon fast asleep. "Now, I'd like to have a word with you," the panther said sternly to Baloo. "Mowgli seems to have Man's ability to get into trouble. The jungle is no place for him. He must go back to the Man-village."

"But I'll take care of him," said the big bear.

"Oh yes? Like you did when the monkeys kidnapped him?" sneered Bagheera. "Besides, sooner or later he's bound to meet Shere Khan, and he hates Man with a vengeance, you know that. He fears Man's gun and Man's fire, and he'll get Mowgli while he's young and helpless. Just one swipe . . ."

Baloo winced. He understood what the panther meant and agreed to tell Mowgli. Bagheera was sure that the Man-cub would listen to his new friend, and he left them alone together.

16

Baloo gently woke Mowgli, and as they set off into the jungle, told him that he had to take him to the Man-village. Mowgli was so upset that he ran straight off into the jungle before Baloo could stop him. Baloo yelled after him, but he was gone. Bagheera heard Baloo's cries and feared the worst.

"If anything happens to that Man-cub, I'll never forgive myself," said Baloo.

"We've got to find him. Let's separate!" yelled Bagheera, charging off into the jungle. He didn't get far before he came across the elephant patrol again. He had some trouble stopping them as they marched through the jungle, but at last he was able to get Colonel Hathi to listen.

"I need your help, Colonel," said Bagheera. "It's an emergency. The Man-cub has gone missing. He's all alone in the jungle!"

Unfortunately for Bagheera, he had no way of knowing that his pleas were being overheard by another animal lurking in the undergrowth nearby. It was Shere Khan, the tiger!

"A lost Man-cub!" said the tiger to himself. "How delightful!"

At first Colonel Hathi was unwilling to help, but finally the

baby elephant managed to persuade him. "Please, father," the little one piped up, "the Man-cub is my friend." This was too much for the Colonel, who immediately dispatched the whole herd in search of Mowgli.

Shere Khan chuckled to himself, and sneaked off into the undergrowth.

Now it seemed that everyone was looking for Mowgli. But the first to spot him was Kaa, the sneaky snake. He quickly wrapped himself round the boy and pulled him up into a tree. "Ssso nice to sssee you again," hissed Kaa. He tried to send Mowgli into a trance, but this time he was interrupted by someone pulling on his tail at the bottom of the tree. It was Shere Khan!

20

"I'd like a word with you," said the tiger with a false smile. "Did I hear you talking to someone up there in the tree?"

"Oh no," replied Kaa, "just talking to myself!"

"You're quite sure you haven't seen the Man-cub, the one who's lost?" asked Shere Khan.

"Man-cub? Oh no!" laughed Kaa uneasily.

"Well, if you do happen to see him, you will inform me at once!" Shere Khan ordered, placing a sharp claw under Kaa's chin. "Understand?"

"I get the point," hissed Kaa, as the tiger walked off. But before he could do anything more, Mowgli pushed him off the tree and he fell to the ground with a thump.

But what was Mowgli to do now? He walked on through the
jungle, and at last he just sat down and cried.

A group of mangy-looking vultures watched him. They
weren't used to seeing a living creature in this part of the
jungle, and they couldn't help feeling sorry for the poor little
boy who looked so sad. They flew down to try and cheer him
up, but Mowgli told them to go away. "Oh, come on," said
Flaps, "we'd like to be your friends."

"We may look a bit shabby, but we've got hearts," said
Buzzie.

"And feelings too," added Dizzy.

Suddenly Shere Khan emerged from the undergrowth. "Bravo! A most moving performance," sneered the tiger.

"Run, friend, run!" Buzzie shouted to Mowgli as the vultures flew off.

"Run? Why should I run?" said Mowgli.

"Why should you run?" laughed Shere Khan. "Is it possible you don't know who I am?"

"I know you, all right," replied Mowgli. "But you don't scare me."

This made Shere Khan angry. He was about to leap at
Mowgli, but something held him back by the tail. It was
Baloo! "Run, Mowgli!" yelled the bear. But still Mowgli
wouldn't do as he was told. Shere Khan chased around with
Baloo holding on to his tail. As the tiger got near Mowgli, the
vultures swooped down and carried the boy off.

24

At that moment lightning struck a tree and it started to burn. The vultures dropped to the ground with Mowgli.

"Fire! That's the only thing the tiger's afraid of!" yelled Buzzie. Mowgli picked up a burning branch and ran towards Shere Khan. The tiger took a swipe at Baloo and knocked him out. The vultures dived down and attacked him, and while he was busy fighting them off, Mowgli tied the burning branch to his tail.

"Look behind you!" crowed Dizzy.

"Y-E-O-W!!!" screamed the tiger, running off into the distance as fast as he could, always followed by the burning branch. Shere Khan was gone for good.

Mowgli went to help Baloo, but found Bagheera standing over him. The bear was lying on the ground, motionless. "Now you've got to be brave, Mowgli, like Baloo was," said Bagheera gently. "He laid down his life for his friend, and Baloo's bravery will forever be engraved on our hearts."

"Beautiful!" sighed Baloo, opening his eyes.

"Baloo, you're all right!" cried Mowgli.

"You old fraud," chuckled Bagheera.

Soon the three friends were heading back through the jungle. As they rested near a river bank, Mowgli heard someone singing nearby. It was a young girl fetching water from the river. "What's that over there?" Mowgli asked Bagheera.

"Oh, it's the Man-village," the panther replied.

Mowgli couldn't take his eyes off the girl. "I've never seen anyone like *that* before," he said.

Bagheera and Baloo watched as Mowgli went closer to the
girl. She saw his reflection in the water and started back
towards the village. But as she went, she dropped the water jug
and it rolled down to Mowgli at the river's edge. He picked up
the jug, re-filled it and followed the girl to the village gate.

Mowgli looked back at his friends. Baloo waved at him to come back, but Bagheera waved him on. Mowgli looked at the girl, turned and followed her into the village.

"Now the Man-cub is back where he belongs," said Bagheera.

Baloo looked at him. "Well, we'd better get back where we belong," he said.

The two friends made their way slowly back into the jungle. They knew that they would never forget the boy named Mowgli and their adventures together.